Where Is Baby?

To Jake and his big sister, Emma
And once again to Steve
—K. O. G.

For my wife Catherine who gives so much
without a thought for herself
—J. B.

Published by
PEACHTREE PUBLISHERS
1700 Chattahoochee Avenue
Atlanta, Georgia 30318-2112
www.peachtree-online.com

Illustrations created in acrylic and colored pencil. Title and by-
lines typeset in Palatino Infant; text typeset in Century School-
book Infant.

Printed in April 2013 by RR Donnelley & Sons in China
10 9 8 7 6 5 4 3 2 1
First Edition

Library of Congress Cataloging-in-Publication Data

Galbraith, Kathryn Osebold.
  Where is baby? / text by Kathryn Galbraith ; illustrations by John
Butler.
    pages cm
  ISBN 978-1-56145-707-6 / 1-56145-707-8
  1. Animals—Infancy—Juvenile literature. 2. Animal defenses—
Juvenile literature. I. Butler, John, 1952- , illustrator. II. Title.
  QL763.G347 2013
  591.3'92—dc23
            2012033522

Where Is Baby?

Kathryn O. Galbraith

Illustrated by John Butler

Ω
PEACHTREE
ATLANTA

Where is baby?

Beneath the blanket?
Under the table?
Behind the chair?
In the hallway?
Up the stairs?

Some babies are found
in unusual places.

Baby deer disappear in dappled spring sunlight.

Baby rabbits freeze in the tall meadow grass.

Baby robins hunch down and don't make a peep.

Baby leopards scramble up high in the trees.

Baby river otters duck and dive without a splash.

Baby polar bears vanish in the snow.

Baby elephants fade behind a forest of legs.

Baby prairie dogs pop down in their holes.

Baby wolves dash into their dens.

Baby bats hang by the hundreds
in quiet, dark caves.

Baby ostriches crouch with
their heads pressed to the ground.

But all babies,

No matter where
they are—

over,

under,

up or down—

never need to worry.

Mama knows
just where
to find them!

More About Babies

A baby deer is called a fawn. Fawns can stand on their long, slender legs and walk just ten minutes after they are born.

A baby rabbit is called a kitten or a kit. A kit is hairless and blind when it is born; it opens its eyes when it is ten days old.

A baby robin is called a chick. When a robin chick is born, it weighs less than a quarter coin.

A baby leopard is called a cub. A leopard mother hides her cubs after they're born, until they are old enough to learn to hunt.

A baby otter is called a pup. A pup is afraid of water when it is first born. It learns to swim by itself when it is about three months old.

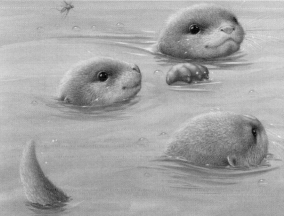

A baby polar bear is called a cub. A cub weighs about a pound when it is born, but will grow to be 650 to 1400 pounds when it is an adult.

A baby elephant is called a calf. When a calf is born, it is already a very big baby. It weighs about 250 pounds and drinks three gallons of mother's milk each day—48 cups!

A baby prairie dog is called a pup. Usually three to five pups are born at the same time. A pup doesn't leave its burrow until it is six weeks old.

A baby bat is called a pup. When it is time for a pup to be born, its mother hangs with her head up and catches her baby in a part of her wing.

A baby wolf is called a pup. Wolves live together in a group called a pack. When the pack goes hunting, one wolf stays behind to babysit the pups.

A baby ostrich is called a chick or a whelp. One giant ostrich egg weighs about three pounds, or as much as twenty-four chicken eggs.

A human newborn is called a baby. A baby can recognize the sound and smell of its mother at birth but cannot recognize her by sight for about six weeks.